WHO ARE YOU?

Stella Blackstone & Debbie Harter

ABBEVILLE KIDS
A Division of Abbeville Publishing Group
New York London Paris

First published in Great Britain in 1996 by Barefoot Books Ltd.

First published in the United States of America in 1996 by
Abbeville Press, 488 Madison Avenue, New York, NY 10022.

Graphic design: DW Design, London

Printed and bound in Belgium

First edition
10 9 8 7 6 5 4 3 2 1

ISBN 0-7892-0291-3

who
are
you?

I'm a bat

who
are
you?

I'm a whale

who
are
you?

who
are
you?

I'm a hare

who
are
you?

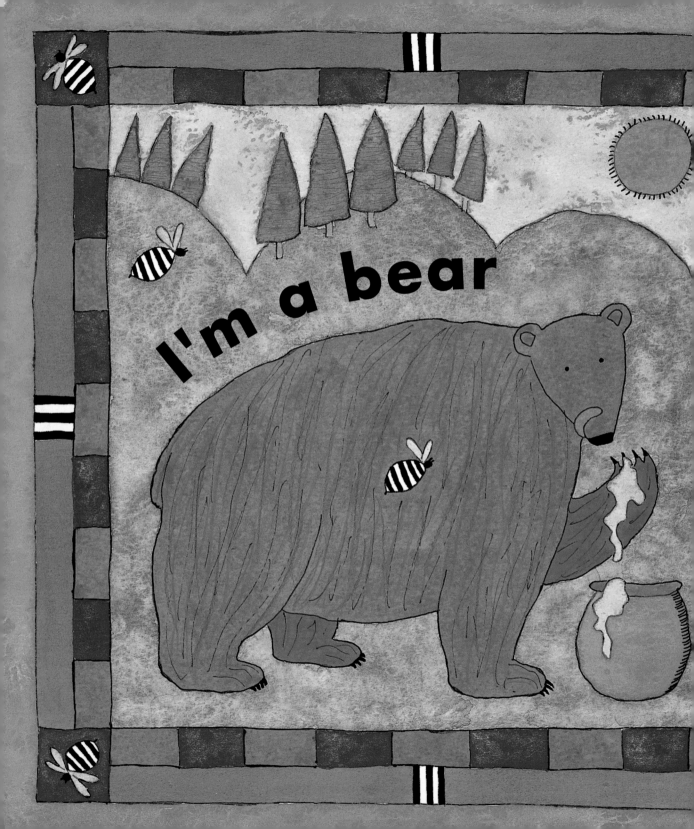

who
are
you?

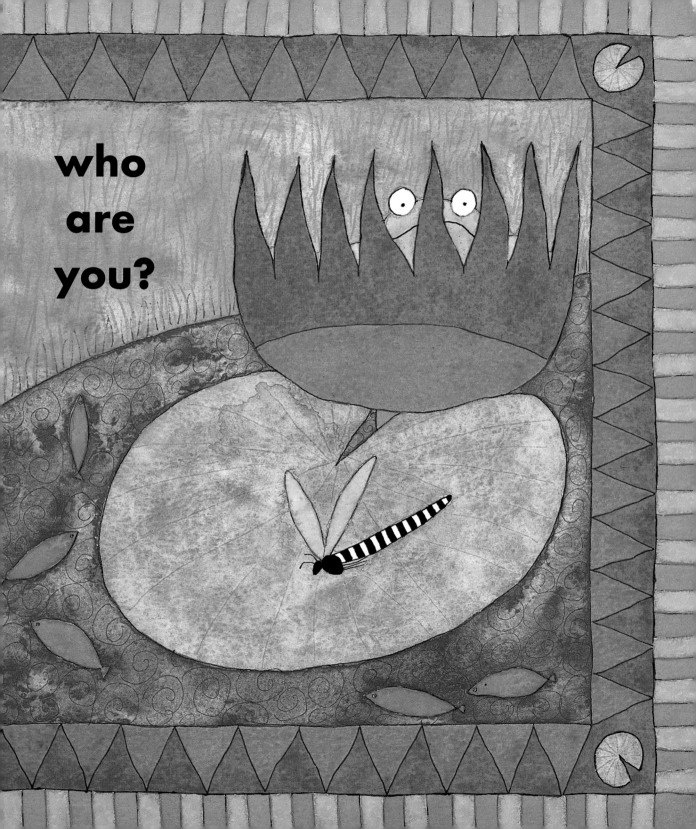

who
are
you?

I'm a frog

who
are
you?

I'm a goose

who
are
you?

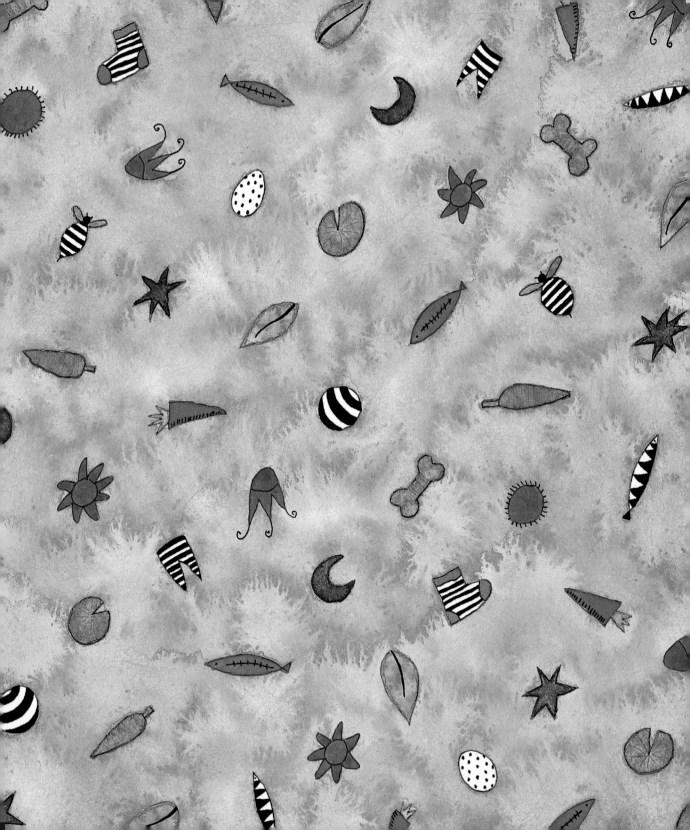